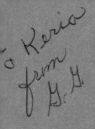

W9-BTR-898

What Will It Be, Penelope?

Written by
Tori Corn

Illustrated by
Danielle Ceccolini

Sky Pony Press
New York

To Shawn, Ellery, Jason, and Zachary with love. —T. C.

Special thanks to Abigail Burns. —D. C.

Text Copyright © 2013 by Tori Corn
Illustrations Copyright © 2013 by Danielle Ceccolini

Sky Pony Press books may be purchased in bulk at special discounts for sales promotion, corporate gifts, fundraising, or educational purposes. Special editions can also be created to specifications. For details, contact the Special Sales Department, Sky Pony Press, 307 West 36th Street, 11th Floor, New York, NY 10018 or info@ skyhorsepublishing.com.

Sky Pony® is a registered trademark of Skyhorse Publishing, Inc.®, a Delaware corporation.

Visit our website at www.skyponypress.com.

10 9 8 7 6 5 4 3 2 1

Library of Congress Cataloging-in-Publication Data

Corn, Tori.
What will it be, Penelope? / written by Tori Corn ; illustrated by Danielle Ceccolini.
p. cm.
Summary: Penelope has a very hard time making a decision about anything, but when her family and friends start choosing everything for her she decides she must change her ways.
ISBN 978-1-62087-542-1 (hardcover : alk. paper) [1. Decision making--Fiction. 2. Family life--Fiction.] I. Ceccolini, Danielle, ill. II. Title.
PZ7.C816342Wh 2013
(E)--dc23
2012041021

ISBN 978-1-62087-542-1
Printed in India

A very special thank you to Julie Matysik for finding a home for Penelope, a big thanks to my agent Liza Fleissig for always believing, and last, but not least, thanks to the incomparable Jill Davis for all of her support.

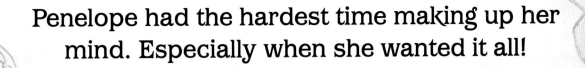

Penelope had the hardest time making up her mind. Especially when she wanted it all!

"What will it be, Penelope?"

"I'll take these!"

"Pick one," said her mother.

But she couldn't. So, Penelope left the store empty-handed.

Deciding what to
eat for breakfast
was difficult.

Getting dressed was nearly impossible.

"I love polka dots, but purple is my favorite color."

"This boa is perfect!"

"You need to get dressed before your friend Eliza comes," said Penelope's mother.

"Rhinestone shoes are stunning, but these sneakers are comfy."

"Hmm . . . should I wear purple or green socks?"

Now that Penelope was dressed, she still had to decide how to wear her hair!

Once Eliza arrived, Penelope didn't know what to play with first.

"Let's play with my dolls. Or, maybe we should have a tea party? Wait . . . let's go outside!" said Penelope.

Once outside, there were even more choices . . .

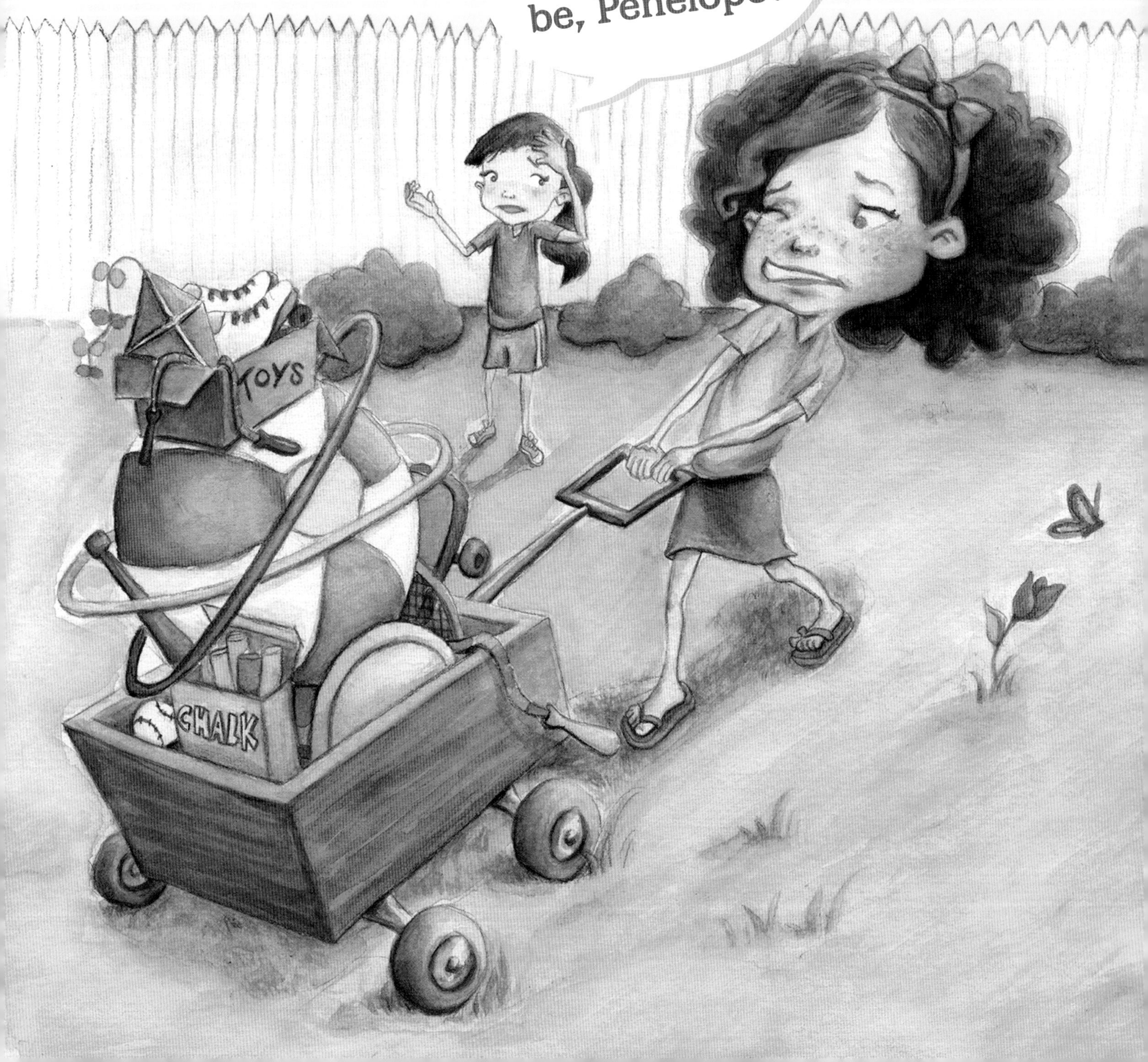

Penelope just couldn't make up her mind,
and Eliza was tired of waiting.

"I'm digging
for worms!"

When Penelope couldn't decide,
someone else did it for her.

"You can wear this today,"
said her mother.

Soon, Penelope wasn't making
any decisions at all.

"We'll read this
book tonight,"
said her grandma.

"We'll take the
black balloon,"
said her father.

"We'll take these,"
said her mother.

Now, whenever Eliza came over,
she got to decide everything.

"Let's play in the attic!"
said Eliza.

One day, Penelope had trouble figuring out which flavor ice cream she wanted.

"There are so many choices!"

Finally, her father decided for her.

Penelope wasn't in the mood for strawberry ice cream.

"I want vanilla ice cream with rainbow sprinkles."

But her father said it was too late.

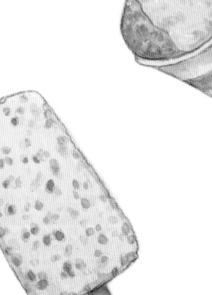

Penelope had
a meltdown.

So did her
ice cream.

And, so, she did.

Some of her decisions were right.

"This tastes yummy!"

And some of her
decisions were wrong.

"I don't need a bathing suit!"

Some of Penelope's decisions were silly and a little strange, but they were hers.

"I've named him Goggles!"

"I say we play with Harold!"
said Penelope.

Now Penelope liked making decisions.

"Do you want some
chicken or a hot dog?"
said her mother.

"Or would you like
one of my special tofu burgers
topped with bean sprouts?"
said her grandma.

"I'd like a hot dog, please!" said Penelope.

And when other people couldn't make up
their mind, Penelope decided for them.

"Make that two hot dogs!" said Penelope.

That night, Penelope was having a ball with Goggles.

"Pleeease, can we stay up a little longer?"

"Not tonight," said her father. "Not all decisions are yours to make."

So, Penelope put on her pajamas, brushed her teeth, and got into bed.

"Would you like a hug or a kiss?" asked her parents. "What will it be?"

"Both!" said Penelope.

It was one decision she didn't need to make!

The End